# The Dragon's Hoard

### Stories from the Viking Sagas

Written by Lari Don

Illustrated by Cate James

**Frances Lincoln**
**Children's Books**

# Contents

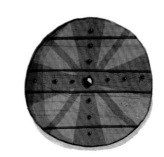

To Viggo – lots of swords and monsters, all for you! - L.D.

For William and James and Thomas and Harry - C.J.

JANETTA OTTER-BARRY BOOKS

Text copyright © Lari Don 2016
Illustrations copyright © Cate James 2016

The rights of Lari Don and Cate James to be identified as the author and illustrator
of this work have been asserted by them in accordance with the Copyright, Designs and
Patents Act, 1988 (United Kingdom).

First published in Great Britain and in the USA in 2016 by Frances Lincoln Children's Books,
74-77 White Lion Street, London N1 9PF
QuartoKnows.com
Visit our blogs at QuartoKnows.com

A catalogue record for this book is available from the British Library.

ISBN 978-1-84780-681-9

Illustrated with pen, ink and digital media

Printed in China

1 3 5 7 9 8 6 4 2

# About the Viking Sagas

These are the stories the Vikings told about themselves.

The Viking sagas were mostly written down in Iceland in the 13th and 14th centuries, about events the writers believed had happened several centuries earlier. Some sagas tell stories from history, some tell ancient myths and legends, but they all tell stories the Icelanders believed had happened to their own ancestors. Stories that were often set far from Iceland, in North America, the British Isles, all over Scandinavia and mainland Europe.

The first saga story I discovered was the story of the Vikings invading Scotland and how they were opposed by the chieftain of Moray. Reading that story was quite an odd experience, because it's from the Orkneyinga Saga, the tales of the Norse Earls of Orkney, which was written with the Earls as the heroes. But I grew up in Moray, so I didn't see the story of Vikings invading Scotland as a magnificent heroic story at all. When I started to tell that story to audiences of children in schools and libraries, I used the information from the saga, but I told it in my own way.

Telling the story of Tusker versus the Earl gave me a taste for reading more sagas. I did enjoy the action-packed stories, but I also decided that the Vikings' violent reputation is probably entirely deserved, and it's possibly even a reputation they were proud of, because they celebrate violence in most of the stories they told about themselves and the ancestors they admired.

However, not all Vikings were violent warriors and raiders, or at least not all the time. They were also farmers, sailors, traders and explorers, and they believed in magic, monsters and ghosts, so I've tried to reflect that variety in the stories I've chosen to retell here.

There's good reason to believe that most of the tales in the sagas were told out loud for many years before they were written down. The stories I retell in this collection are the versions I tell out loud to audiences, which means they're not exactly as they appear in the sagas. I'm not a historian, a translator or an academic. I just love to share these stories from the sagas, and they change a little as I tell them, just as the original oral tales will have changed as they were told.

This is not a fact book; this is a book of stories. The Vikings loved fighting and sailing and feasting, but they also loved storytelling.

I hope you enjoy their stories too.

Lari Don

# The Dragon's Hoard

from The Saga of the Volsungs

Loki, the Viking god of mischief, often caused trouble deliberately. But one morning he caused trouble entirely by accident.

He was walking by the river when a glossy otter scrambled out of the water, dragging a plump salmon. Loki wanted the salmon for his breakfast and knew the otter's fur would be valuable.

So he crept up and killed the otter, with one swift blow to the head.

Before he could roast the fish or skin the otter, a group of men ran towards the river from a nearby cave. "That's our brother! You've killed our brother!"

"This isn't a man," said Loki, "this is an otter."

"Our brother was a shape-shifter, so when he wanted to fish, he became an otter. You've killed our brother and you must pay!"

Loki agreed he must pay. In the Viking world, if you paid compensation for a death, even a deliberate killing, then it wasn't murder. So Loki gave the brothers a generously huge pile of gold, then walked away with a grin, the fish dangling from his hand.

But the glittering gold Loki left behind didn't bring anyone good fortune.

One of the brothers, Fafnir, loved the gold.

Fafnir piled the gold in his corner of the cave. He ran his fingers through it. He sat on it. He lay on it. He rolled in it. He curled up round it to sleep. He growled at his own brothers, if they came near the gold.

Soon Fafnir began to turn into a dragon, to guard the gold.

He grew bigger and heavier, he grew claws and fangs and rock-hard scales on his back. But he still had a soft skin-covered belly, so he could feel the gold when he slept on it.

Eventually the dragon drove his brothers from their home. Fafnir lived alone in his dragon's cave, lying on his dragon's hoard.

Fafnir guarded the gold with his claws, his fangs and his poisonous breath. His toxic breath burnt the leaves off trees and killed any person it touched. When the dragon left his cave to drink at the river, he breathed on anyone who stood in his way, then ate them.

The story of the dragon and his golden hoard was told at feasts and in marketplaces, and the story was heard by a young hero called Sigurd….

Though Sigurd wasn't really a hero. His father had been a hero, but Sigurd hadn't done anything heroic yet. Sigurd decided the perfect way to start his hero's career was to kill a dragon and take its gold.

He visited the blacksmith's forge and asked for a sword. The blacksmith offered him the standard hero sword and Sigurd tested the blade by swinging it at the smith's huge black anvil.

The sword shattered.

"I'll need a better sword than that, to defeat a dragon. Can you make me your best-ever sword?"

The smith laboured over the perfect blade.

When it was finished, Sigurd swung it against the anvil.

The sword shattered.

The smith shrugged. "I can't make a stronger sword than that."

Sigurd went home and found his father's sword, which had been given to his father by the god, Odin and had broken against Odin's spear on the day his father died. Sigurd took the broken blade to the forge and the smith joined the halves together. Sigurd swung it at the anvil, and the sword sliced right through the black metal.

"This sword is fit for a hero facing a dragon!"

But the hero couldn't face the dragon, Sigurd realised, as he sat on the hill above the cave, and watched the dragon stomp down to the river for a drink. He couldn't attack the dragon from the front, because he would be burnt by that poisonous breath. He couldn't ambush the dragon from the back or sides either, because those scales were too hard even for his sword.

Sigurd came up with a plan.

He visited the blacksmith one more time and asked for a spade. Sigurd returned to the dragon's lair, waited until the dragon was asleep on the gold, and then dug a pit in the path between the cave and the river. Then he crouched at the bottom of the pit, with his sword on his right and his spade on his left.

After hours of crouching in the cold damp pit, Sigurd felt the ground shake. He heard the thump of heavy clawed feet. He heard the dragon's mutters and growls. He saw the dragon's spiky head pass above him. Then the pit turned completely black, as the massive bulk of the dragon's body blocked out the sky.

Sigurd grasped his sword and thrust it upwards, through the dragon's soft belly, into the dragon's heart.

The dragon roared! The dragon's blood flowed into the pit. Sigurd rolled out of the way, but three drops of blood landed on his lips. As soon as the dragon's

blood touched his lips, Sigurd could understand words in the roars of pain above him.

"I am dying!" roared Fafnir. "I'm dying and it's all the fault of that gold. Loki's gold drove away my family, and now it's cost me my life. I hope it brings the same fortune to my killer."

The dragon gasped a final breath and fell heavily to the ground, right on top of the pit. The dragon's body covered the pit entirely, like a lid on a pot.

Now Sigurd was trapped in a hole by the dragon he'd just slain!

But he still had his spade. So he dug a tunnel out of the pit. Then he wiped the blood and mud from his hands and entered the cave.

Despite the dragon's final words, Sigurd claimed all the gold. "How else," he said, "can I prove I'm the hero who killed the dreaded Fafnir?"

As he left the cave with the gold, he realised the dragon's blood had given him the power to understand the speech of birds, as well as the speech of dragons. Birds, he discovered, mainly talk about worms and seeds and the weather. Though they do sometimes hear useful gossip.

The dragon's gold brought Sigurd a hero's fame, but it didn't bring him good fortune. Because of that gold, the blacksmith plotted to kill him, he fell in love with a woman sleeping behind an inconvenient ring of flames, and he drank a witch's potion that made him forget everything important.

In his fairly short life (heroes don't live long), Sigurd gained more good fortune from the words of birds than he ever did from the dragon's hoard of gold. Perhaps gold given by the god of mischief is always more trouble than it's worth.

# The Swan Warrior

from The Saga of Hromund Gripsson

Once there was a warrior called Helgi the Bold, who was preparing to follow his king into battle. He tried to say goodbye to Kara, the girl he loved.

"Why do you have to fight this battle?" she asked.

"I'm a warrior, pledged to fight for my king."

"But you've fought for him so often. I thought you were going to stay here and settle down with me."

"I will, some day, but I've promised to stand in the shieldwall for this battle."

"I'll follow you and protect you," said Kara, "if you promise it will be your last battle."

Helgi grinned. "I promise it will be my last battle, but how could you protect me?" He looked down at Kara, six inches shorter than him and half as wide.

"This is how I will protect you." Kara fetched a white feather cloak from her house, then wrapped the cloak round her shoulders. As she raised her arms, they became wide white wings. A swan rose into the air and flew around Helgi, then landed on the ground and became a girl with a feather cloak in her arms. "That is how I will protect you."

Helgi had known Kara since they were children, but he'd never realised she

was a sorceress. "You make a beautiful swan, my darling, but how can a swan protect me against enemy blades?"

"I will fly above the battle, singing a spell to protect you against all weapons. So long as you can hear my song, you'll be safe. And after this battle you must put away your weapons. Then we can settle down on a farm and raise a family."

So Helgi joined the war party travelling to the battlefield by the shores of Lake Vanern, and Kara flew above them all the way.

Warriors on both sides held their shields up, overlapping them to create a long wall of shields. The men at the front readied their swords and the men at the back readied their spears and their bows and arrows.

The two opposing shieldwalls faced each other. The warriors walked towards each other. Then they ran towards each other. The shieldwalls crashed hard against each other.

The battle began.

Kara flew high in the sky, singing. She sang a deep slow song, weaving a spell of protection around Helgi, so nothing could hurt him.

As Helgi fought, jabbing below and above the shieldwall, he saw an arrow curve away from his shoulder (and hit the man next to him) and a spear jerk away above his helmet (and hit the man behind him). He grinned and he fought.

Kara sang, loud and powerful, to keep the spell of protection strong.

The battle raged below her.

As injured warriors fell away, the shieldwalls fell apart. The battle became man against man, warrior against warrior, lots of small intense life-or-death duels.

Helgi fought on, protected from every blade by the swan above. Sure of her protection, he dropped his shield, so he could move faster and fight with two weapons.

Helgi fought. Kara sang. The battle raged.

But battles are noisy, with the smash of shields, the crash of weapons and the screams of the wounded. Kara flew lower, so she could be sure Helgi heard her song.

Helgi was fighting better than he'd ever fought before. He fought with the confidence of a warrior who knew nothing could hurt him, and he stabbed and slashed and defeated warriors all around.

Kara flew lower as the battle got noisier. Warriors were now shouting battle cries: the names of their gods or their fathers or their favourite swords.

Helgi was yelling a new battle cry at the top of his voice: "I am the Swan Warrior and nothing can touch me!"

Kara flew lower and lower, singing louder and louder, so Helgi could still hear her. As she flew nearer the battle, the swan had to dodge arrows and spears. She couldn't sing a spell of protection for herself at the same time as protecting Helgi.

Helgi could still hear her song, and he knew she was up there, protecting him. But he didn't look up, he looked ahead, he looked into the eyes of the men he fought.  And he yelled his Swan Warrior battle cry.

Kara flew even lower, still singing her song.

Helgi lifted his sword to attack the next warrior in his way. He stepped forward and slashed the sword upwards to bring it down onto his enemy's head.

The point of his sword cut right through the belly of the swan above him.

Kara fell to the ground. Her song fell silent.

Suddenly Helgi wasn't protected any more. He didn't even have his shield. Nothing could save him from the blades of the brothers of all the men he had killed.

So that was Helgi's last battle.

Kara and Helgi never settled down together on a farm, but they did stay together forever. They're still lying beside each other on that old battlefield.

# The Berserker's Baby

from The Vatnsdal Saga

Thorir was a berserker.

Berserkers were the most feared of all Viking warriors. They lost control completely when they were fighting. They felt no concern for their own safety, they just flung themselves into the heart of the fight. At the start of a battle, they were often seen biting their own shields in their impatience to get at the enemy.

Some people even said berserkers changed into bears or wolves in battle, because they fought like animals.

Thorir was tired of being a berserker. He didn't like feeling out of control, he didn't like losing his mind and wanting nothing but rage and blood and death. He wanted to know who he was when he fought. So he consulted the wise women and the elders of his family, but no one knew a way to stop being a berserker.

One day, Thorir was walking home through the hills when he heard a thin wailing cry. It was so different from his own deafening yells as he flung himself at a shieldwall of enemies, that he decided to investigate.

High on the cold rocks, he found a baby, tightly wrapped in a blanket. The baby was sobbing and scratching at the blanket over its face. Thorir pulled the blanket away, so the baby could breathe. The baby screamed louder.

Thorir sat down beside the baby. This must be a child abandoned to die on the hillside, he thought, because a family was embarrassed by its birth or couldn't afford to feed it.

Thorir looked at the sun far off in the sky and said, "I wish to stop being a berserker. And this baby wishes to live. God of the Sun, if I promise to care for this child, will you lift the curse of being a berserker from my shoulders?"

He took off his bearskin cloak and laid it on the rocks. He felt the sun hot on his shoulders, though it was freezing cold in the hills.

Thorir smiled, picked up the baby and went home. Leaving the bearskin behind him on the hillside.

I don't know if it was the power of the Sun God, or because Thorir was always exhausted after sleepless nights of teething, the strains of potty training and the many worries of a father seeing a son grow up. But Thorir never felt the rage of a berserker again.

The little wailing baby became a warrior called Thorkel the Scratcher. But Thorkel never lost control, he always knew who he was when he fought, and he never chewed on his own shield.

# Tusker versus the Earl

from The Orkneyinga Saga

The first Earl of Orkney was the perfect Viking. His skalds composed poems describing him as tall, blond, handsome, strong… and vicious. The perfect Viking.

Like many Vikings, the first Earl was also greedy. He wasn't content with the fertile islands of Orkney, he wanted more: more land, more wealth, more power. He looked south, at Scotland, and he wanted it.

So he invaded, with his army of Vikings.

He conquered Caithness and Cromarty, and moved south through Scotland, his vicious Viking warriors destroying any resistance. Then they came to Moray, and met a man who could stop them.

Maelbrigte was the chieftain of Moray, and his bards didn't describe him as blond and handsome. He had wild crinkly red hair and long squint yellow teeth. One front tooth stuck out over his lip like a boar's tusk, so even his friends called him Tusker.

Maelbrigte Tusker was a great warrior, and under his leadership the men of Moray stopped the Viking invasion and held them at the borders of Moray.

But Tusker's men could only stop the invaders' advance, they couldn't drive the Vikings back to Orkney.

While the armies fought day after day, the farmers couldn't harvest their crops and the people began to starve. Neither side was winning, so the skalds on one side and the bards on the other suggested a truce, to discuss peace.

The skalds and bards agreed that the two leaders would meet at dawn the next day, on the hills above the Moray Firth. To make sure that neither leader would have an advantage and therefore neither leader would be likely to start a fight, they agreed that each leader would arrive with exactly forty men on exactly forty horses.

But the Earl said to himself, "This is Tusker's land. He could have a man hiding behind every clump of heather. That's what I'd do. It would be stupid to bring only forty men." So he decided to take the agreed forty horses, but put two men on each horse. Forty horses, and eighty men.

Tusker might be scary when he smiled and he rarely brushed his teeth, but he was an honest man. The next morning he led forty men on forty horses to the hillside. Just as he had agreed.

As the mist rose up off the land, the Moray chief saw the legs of forty horses across the heather. Then the mist rose higher, and he saw the feet of the men on the horses. He frowned. The mist rose higher still, and he saw the legs of the men. He realised that there were two legs hanging down on each horse's flank. There were two men on each horse.

Tusker could see forty horses, and eighty men.

He turned to his own men. "I'm sorry. I should never have trusted the word of a Viking. We're outnumbered, and we're going to die here today. But if we have to die, let's take as many of them with us as we can, so there are fewer Vikings left to attack our families."

Tusker screamed a war cry and before the mist was even up above their heads, the men of Moray charged straight at the Vikings.

The Earl gave a signal, and one man leapt off each horse, to run round behind the men of Moray as they charged. So Tusker's men faced foes on horseback, and were also attacked by men on foot from behind.

The men of Moray were outnumbered and surrounded, but they were fighting on their own land for their own families' freedom, and they fought hard.

Suddenly the two sides pulled apart, to watch a duel. Tusker and the Earl were off their horses, facing each other in the middle of the battleground.

First Tusker and the Earl fought with words.

"I should never have trusted the promise of a Viking, of a sea-raider, a pirate, a murderer and a thief," called Maelbrigte Tusker. "You learn to lie through your teeth in your mother's arms."

The Earl laughed. "I may lie through my teeth, but at least when I smile I don't curdle milk or make babies cry!"

After the insults came the first few testing blows.

Both men were expert swordsmen. But it wasn't a fair fight. The battle hadn't been a fair fight because the Earl had put two men on each horse, and this duel wasn't a fair fight because Tusker was already injured. The tendons behind his right knee had been slashed by one of the Vikings on foot, so he couldn't put much weight on it and he couldn't move fast. And in a duel, moving fast is what counts.

Tusker parried and thrust and fought with all his skill, and the Earl's blows couldn't get past his strong shield-arm and his swift sword-arm. Then the Earl realised Tusker couldn't move fast on his feet, and the Earl grinned.

He leapt behind the Moray chief, and before Tusker could limp round to face him, the Earl threw down his shield, put both hands on his long sword, and swung it high and fast.

He cut off Maelbrigte Tusker's head.

As Tusker's red head bounced on the ground, the Vikings turned on the men of Moray and killed them all.

The Earl bent down, picked up Tusker's head and called to his men, "Cut off all their heads! Tie them to your saddles. Let's show the people of Moray what happens to anyone who defies the Earl of Orkney!"

He tied a strand of Maelbrigte's long curly hair to his saddle, so the severed head bounced on his horse's flank.

As he rode away, the Earl's horse stumbled, and the Earl kicked viciously at his horse's ribs. When he jerked his leg, his knee knocked against Tusker's head. And the long yellow tooth, the tusk that jutted from the Moray chief's mouth, scratched the Earl's leg.

The Earl laughed. "There's no point biting me now, Tusker. You lost. I won. Your people and your lands are all mine!"

But the Earl didn't rule Moray for long.

That night the scratch on the Earl's leg began to itch. The next day it swelled. The day after he became feverish. The night after that he dreamed of eight-legged horses. And the day after that, the Earl died of blood poisoning.

So that is how Maelbrigte Tusker's long yellow tooth defeated the perfect Viking.

# The Bear in Chains

from The Tale of Audun from the West Fjords

The men of the north tell a story about a man and a polar bear. The bears of the north tell a story about a polar bear and a man….

Audun was a young Icelandic man, without much money and with a mother to care for. So he took a job on a cargo ship sailing to Greenland. "When I return," he told his mother, "I will return a rich man."

Audun worked hard for the ship-owner and soon saved enough to buy his own cargo, to make his own fortune.

He chose to buy a polar bear, a young bear captured when its mother was killed. Audun hoped this beautiful white bear would bring him riches. So he wrapped the bear in chains and took it by boat to Norway, spending most of his remaining money on passage across the northern seas.

When he arrived in Norway, Audun was summoned to the king, who had heard of the white bear and its long journey.

"That's a marvellous bear," said the King of Norway.

"Thank you," said Audun. "I plan to give it to the King of Denmark."

The King of Norway frowned. "Why to the King of Denmark, and not to me?"

"Denmark is further from the ice where the white bears live, so this bear will be more unusual and more valuable in Denmark than in Norway."

The King of Norway laughed. "That's a good answer. I won't take offence and I'll grant you safe passage through my lands."

As the bear and Audun travelled south, by land and boat, the bear grew bigger and Audun's purse grew lighter. Eventually, he had no money left to buy food. When they reached the palace of the Danish king, the bear was thin, weak with hunger and wrapped in rusty chains. Audun was also hungry and beginning to wish he had given the bear to the Norwegian king.

Audun knocked on the back door of the palace and asked permission to give a gift to the king. The palace steward said, "You can't give that bear to our king! All dirty and skinny and rusty! We must feed it up and give it a bath, to make it fit for the king. You don't look much better. I suppose I'd better feed you up too."

Audun thanked the steward for his kindness. The steward said it wasn't kindness, he'd only feed them if Audun granted him a half-share in the bear. Audun looked at the starving bear and nodded.

The steward fed them both, then Audun bathed the bear until its fur gleamed white, though its eyes were sad and dull. Audun wrapped shiny new chains round the bear and led it to the throne room. He presented the white bear from the icy north as a gift to the King of Denmark.

The king was delighted with the white bear, though he was angry with his steward for taking advantage of Audun's enterprise. "This young man travelled from the end of the world with this magnificent bear and you tried to steal half of his honour and renown. You deserve nothing but a return to work in the kitchens."

As Audun had hoped, the King of Denmark gave him many gifts to thank him for the wonderful white bear: a bag of silver, a gold armband and a beautiful new ship with red sails, filled with valuable cargo. After a few months as an honoured guest at the palace, Audun sailed home, to make his mother proud and happy.

And that's where the story told by the men of the north ends. But the story told by the bears of the north doesn't stop there....

The bear was locked in a cage in the palace grounds, so the people of Denmark could stare at him. He was too warm, covered in heavy fur designed for colder weather. He was trapped in a small cage, unable to swim or run. He was no longer starving, but he wanted hot salty seal-meat, not dry bread, muddy onions and stringy chicken.

On the day the king waved Audun off in his splendid ship, the steward visited the cage to moan at the bear. The steward complained that despite his cunning in helping Audun, he hadn't been given silver or jewellery or ships.

The steward unlocked the cage door and threw in a rotting cabbage. "That's how we're both treated," he said, "like a stinking cabbage on top of the midden. You in a cage, me in the kitchen."

The steward slouched off back to work, but he didn't lock the cage door as he left. Perhaps he forgot.

The bear slowly pushed the door open and stepped outside. He stood on his hind legs and sniffed. Then he followed the salty scent of the sea towards the harbour, where he saw a ship with red sails heading north.

The bear dived into the sea and followed the ship.

Polar bears are wonderful swimmers. They can swim in icy waters for hundreds of miles. The bear swam behind the ship, all the way to the north islands.  First to Iceland, where Audun showed his mother the king's fine gifts, then to Greenland, where Audun traded his cargo and boasted about his trip to Denmark.

So the white bear followed the ship Audun had been given by the king as thanks for bringing the bear south, and that ship led him back home.  The bear returned to his family and his hunting grounds, with an amazing story to tell.

The King of Denmark never worked out where his magnificent white bear had gone. Only the bears know that the stolen bear came back home… and now you know too!

# The Raven Banner

from The Orkneyinga Saga and Njal's Saga

Once there was a noblewoman called Eithne, whose son was the Earl of Orkney. She hoped her son would make her proud. But one day he came to visit her and said that he'd been challenged to fight a Scottish chieftain who had seven times more men than him, and that he was afraid he would lose. He looked embarrassed as he admitted to his mother that he was afraid he would die.

His mother sighed. "If I thought you would live forever, my son, I would have kept you safe in my sewing basket. But you're a warrior, so you must risk defeat and death."

"You don't want me to lose my first major battle, do you? That wouldn't reflect well on you, Mother."

Eithne laughed, and offered to make him a banner that would bring him victory whenever it was carried at the head of his army.

She stitched a bright banner for the Earl, with the green of the Orkney Islands and the blue of the sea as background, and in the centre a huge black raven, the bird of the battlefield. When the banner fluttered in the wind at the top of its long pole, the raven's wings flapped and the bird seemed to fly.

"This banner will bring victory to the men who march behind it," said Eithne.

"But at a cost, because the banner will also bring death to the man who carries it."

The Earl thanked her and accepted the banner.

As his men approached the Scottish chieftain's force, the Earl asked who would like the honour of carrying his raven banner into battle. A young warrior stepped forward and proudly held the banner high.

The Earl's men won their victory against the Scots, but the young warrior was cut down in the last few moments of fighting.

The Earl marched behind that banner every time he went into battle. The banner brought the Earl many victories, so he brought his mother great wealth and honour. As he told stories of the battles he'd won under her raven banner, Eithne sat and sewed and smiled.

Then the Earl was summoned to fight for the Norse king, against the Irish king. He took his men and his raven banner to the chosen battlefield, near Dublin. As the two sides got ready for the battle, the Earl said to his men, "Who would like the honour of carrying my raven banner this time?"

The Earl's men had enjoyed the victories the banner brought, but they'd also watched the warrior who carried the banner die each time.

They'd started to suspect that carrying the banner was a curse as well as an honour.

So none of the Earl's men stepped forward.

The Earl asked again who would carry his banner.

But the Earl's men concentrated on polishing their helmets and sharpening their swords. None of them looked up and met his eyes.

The Earl realised that no one would ever carry the raven banner for him again.

He thought about going into battle without the banner. He thought about risking defeat, about letting his king down. He thought about going home and telling his mother that he'd failed to use her gift in this most important battle. He thought about what his mother would say.

The Earl said, "It's probably time I carried my own banner."

He held the raven high. And his men ran into battle, the raven's wings flapping ahead of them.

In the very last moments of the battle, one of the Irish warriors stabbed the Earl. As he fell to the ground, the banner fell with him, and the Irish warrior sliced the raven banner into rags.

The Earl's men returned to Orkney to tell Eithne of her son's death, and to give her the bloodstained remains of the raven banner. She put the rags in her sewing basket, and she smiled. She was proud of her son, because he had at last carried his own banner into battle.

# The Boy in the Bones

from The Saga of King Hrolf Kraki

Bodvar was a hero. He knew he was a hero because he had a hero's sword.

He had visited a cave with his two brothers, and they'd found the hilts of three weapons sticking out of the cave wall: a dagger, a short sword and a great long sword. The oldest brother pulled at the long sword, but it was solid in the rock. He was only able to remove the dagger. The middle brother tried the long sword too, but he was only able to remove the short sword. When Bodvar, the youngest brother, put his hand on the long sword, it slid out of the rock easily.

So Bodvar knew he was a hero, with a hero's sword. Now he had to choose what kind of hero he wanted to be, and he decided to serve his king as a warrior. He travelled the length of the country to the king's hall, and on the way he slept in barns, in shepherds' huts and under trees. But on the last night of his journey he was offered shelter by a farmer and his wife. They fed him well and gave him a warm bed. Then they asked him a favour.

"When you reach the king's hall, please look out for our son, Hott. He left home to become a warrior, but he's not very brave, and we're worried about him."

Bodvar promised he would look after Hott, then walked on to the king's hall.

The king welcomed Bodvar's youth and strength and magnificent sword, and invited Bodvar to sit with his warriors at their feast.

Bodvar sat down and ate. But he noticed that, in the corner of the hall, the warriors were laughing and jeering. He strolled over. They were shouting rude comments, and aiming crusts and cutlery at a pile of chewed bones that had been thrown into the corner.

The pile of bones was shaking.

The king's men were sniggering. "What a fine warrior Hott is, shivering in his pile of bones."

Bodvar realised that inside that pile of bones was a boy. The boy he'd promised to look out for.

So Bodvar kicked the pile of bones apart and pulled the boy out.

"Why did you do that?" whispered Hott. "It took me ages to build that shieldwall of bones, and I was safe behind it."

"No warrior should hide like that," said Bodvar. "No man should live like that. I promised your mother I'd take care of you, so sit with me and eat. Tomorrow I will teach you courage."

But it wasn't quite that easy. Hott could hold a wooden sword and he could handle it well when he was practising sword moves. But he trembled and shivered when he faced an actual opponent, even if that opponent was holding another blunt wooden sword.

After a few frustrating days of trying to turn this shaking boy into a warrior, Bodvar noticed one evening that Hott wasn't the only one at the tables who was pale and nervous.

"What's going on?" he asked Hott.

"It's nearly the feast of Yule, and every year at Yule a monster appears for three nights in a row, to kill and eat the king's livestock. It also kills and eats any warrior who tries to stop it. Look, everyone is afraid, not just me."

Suddenly there was a deep rattling roar outside. All the warriors stood up and drew their swords.

"No!" shouted the king. "I can't afford to lose more warriors to this beast. So I forbid you to go out and fight it. Stay safe indoors and let it eat all the animals it wants. I can spare a few sheep, but I can't spare more warriors or I will have no army left to fight for me in the summer. Sit down and ignore the roars."

The warriors breathed quiet sighs of relief and sat down to eat, as the roars continued outside. The warriors lay down to sleep. All except Bodvar, who waited until everyone else was snoring. Then he prodded Hott in the ribs. "Bring a torch, we're going out."

"We can't go out. There's a monster out there."

"That's why we're going out."

"But the king has forbidden anyone to fight the monster."

"I am a hero," said Bodvar, "with a hero's sword, and there is a monster outside. If I hide inside all night, I'll never be a true hero. This is what I'm for."

Bodvar left the hall, followed by Hott carrying a small burning torch. They couldn't see the monster, but they followed the sounds of screaming animals and ripping flesh. Hott was trembling, so the torchlight wavered. But they found the monster, eating a huge white bull. They hid behind a rock and watched.

In the faint and wavering torchlight, they could only see glimpses of the beast. A scaly leg. Sharp teeth in a wide jawbone. Lumpy warts and gleaming spikes. Bloodstained claws.

But those glimpses were enough to make Hott shake even more.

"You stay safe here," said Bodvar. "I'll wait for my moment, then attack."

He waited until the beast was concentrating on crunching the bull's horns. Then Bodvar stood up, walked towards the monster, lifted his magnificent sword and stabbed the beast three times in the heart.

The monster fell down dead.

Bodvar said to Hott, "Help me prop it up against this rock."

Hott helped Bodvar drag the monster to the rock. "Why are we propping it up?"

"Because tomorrow you are going to kill it."

"How can I kill it? You've already killed it. It's already dead."

"No one else knows that," said Bodvar.

They propped the beast up, facing the king's hall, with its wide jaws open and one clawed foot raised.

Then they returned to the hall and fell asleep. They were woken the next morning by someone yelling, "The beast is still here. It didn't leave when the sun came up!" The warriors looked out at the monster, which was staring at the hall, showing all its long sharp fangs, with one clawed foot raised ready to slash and tear.

In the morning light they could see it clearly: a huge beast with the scales of a snake, the warts of a toad, the jaws of a wolf and lots of bone-white spikes. All covered in bull's blood.

The king said, "If this beast is getting bolder and threatening us in the daylight, we must get rid of it. Who will kill it for me?"

Bodvar jabbed Hott in the ribs. "This is your chance."

Hott whispered back, "Can you lend me your hero's sword?"

Bodvar shook his head. "You must ask the king for his royal sword."

Hott took a deep breath and walked towards the king, in front of all the warriors who had bullied him. "I will kill the monster, if you will give me your sword to strike it down."

The king frowned at this skinny boy demanding his sword. But the boy had spoken loudly and clearly, and his hands weren't trembling, so the king smiled. "On you go then, Hott, let's see what you can do."

He gave Hott the long, shining, royal sword.

Hott grasped the hilt in his steady hands, ran out of the hall, sprinted towards the monster and drove the sword into its chest.

The dead monster slid down the rock and lay still at his feet.

The warriors cheered, shouting Hott's name.

After that day, Hott never trembled or shivered. He never hid behind bones. And, standing side by side with Bodvar, he fought and defeated lots of real, live monsters.

# Sailing to America

from The Greenlanders' Saga

*In fourteen hundred and ninety-two, Columbus sailed the ocean blue.*

But almost 500 years before Christopher Columbus sailed to the New World, Vikings sailed across northern oceans much greyer and colder. The Vikings were the first Europeans to discover America.

The first Viking to see North America was a trader called Bjarni Herjolfson, who was blown off course when he was sailing from Iceland to Greenland. He saw strange lands much further west than any Norse ships had ever been, but he didn't land because, as soon as the wind changed, he sailed straight back home.

When he told the King of Norway about the lands far to the west, the king asked, "What people live there? What king rules there? What grows there? Can profits be made there?"

But Bjarni couldn't tell him, because Bjarni had stayed on board his ship.

The king was disappointed. "Why didn't you explore?"

The trader shrugged. He'd simply wanted to get back to familiar waters.

So a sailor called Leif Eiriksson, who was keen to satisfy the king's curiosity, signed up a crew of 35 men and sailed to the west of Greenland to see what he could find.

He found a rocky, icy coast, which he named Helluland. He sailed south and named the forested coast they found next Markland, then he named the fertile green coast even further south Vinland.

Leif and his crew left their ship and explored these new lands. They stayed long enough in Vinland to cut wood and harvest grapes, and no matter how far they explored, they didn't see any people at all.

They returned home with their wood and grapes, with answers to some of the king's questions and with the honour of being the first Norsemen to set foot on this western land.

The next year, Leif's brother Thorvald took the ship and a crew back to Vinland to explore further. As they sailed along the shore, Thorvald saw a beautiful piece of land jutting out into the sea, with a white beach and fine trees.

Thorvald said to his crew, "I want to make my home there, in that peaceful place. I will be the first of our people to live in this land. But first let's sail on and see what else we can discover."

Later that day, Thorvald and his men hauled their ship up onto a long shallow beach and went exploring. As they walked far along the shoreline, they noticed three smooth humps on the sand. Were they rocks? Or beached whales? The Vikings walked closer, prodded them, and realised that the humps were boats.

The Vikings flipped over the three skin canoes and found three men hiding under each one. All nine men leapt up and ran.

Thorvald and his men were surprised that other people had already made their home on this land, because Leif had told them no one lived here. But their surprise didn't stop the Vikings attacking.

They chased, grabbed and killed the men. When they counted the bodies on the sand, they realised they'd only killed eight men. One man had got away.

"Back to the ship!" ordered Thorvald.

It was too late. The man who'd escaped was already returning, with reinforcements. He was paddling down the coast leading a swarm of canoes. As the Vikings ran down the long beach towards their ship, the men in the canoes fired arrows at them.

The Vikings ran as fast as they could, with the arrows whirring and buzzing past them. They all carried swords and axes, but those weapons were designed for close combat, and were no use against enemies attacking from a distance.

When they reached their ship, Thorvald boosted each of his men up the wooden hull, before clambering up himself. As soon as the Vikings were all on the ship, sheltering behind the shields lining the gunwale, the men in canoes turned round and paddled away.

"Anyone hurt?" gasped Thorvald.

Every one of his crew said, "No."

Thorvald raised his arm to show an arrow sticking out between his ribs. "I'm hit," he said. He began to cough, then slid to the deck. "I'm hit and I'm dying. But I still want to make this new land my home. Bury me on that beautiful headland and I can stay here for ever."

So his crew buried Thorvald on the headland and he stayed there when his ship sailed away.

Thorvald Eirikson was the first European to make his home in North America, and his bones lay there for almost 500 years before Christopher Columbus thought of sailing the ocean blue.

The sagas tell us about the Vikings' explorations of North America, but no saga can tell us what the men in skin boats thought of those first invaders. Though perhaps those arrows sent a fairly clear message.

# Zombie on the Roof

from Grettir's Saga

Once upon a time there was a farm. And some zombies.

The farm was called Thorhallsstead, in Iceland, and it had a reputation for being haunted by ghosts. Viking ghosts weren't pale, see-through, wifty-wafty shapes moaning 'oooh' and drifting through walls. Viking ghosts were solid and strong, formed of the bodies of the unquiet dead. Nowadays we would call them zombies.

Because his farm had the reputation of being haunted by the dangerous, smelly, living dead, the farmer Thorhall found it difficult to attract farmworkers. However, one autumn, a man called Glam applied for the job as Thorhallsstead's shepherd.

"You do know the farm is haunted?" asked Thorhall.

Glam nodded. "That's fine. Life would be a bit boring without the occasional haunting."

So Glam started to care for the farm's sheep. But one evening, he didn't return with the flock.

In the morning Thorhall and his sons searched the hills. They found the scattered sheep, and they found Glam's body. He'd been killed, possibly by trolls, possibly by ghosts. But he was definitely dead.

They tried to carry his body to the churchyard for burial, but his body refused to be moved. It became too heavy to lift, or it vanished when they looked away, or it even fought back.

So they buried the body in the hills, under a mound of stones. But Glam didn't lie easy in his grave. He rose up and haunted the farm every night.

And Glam was the worst ghost they'd ever had, because he was a fresh corpse, in a bad mood.

Glam wanted to return to the warmth of the farmhouse. So every night he tried the doors and the windows, which were always barred and blocked. When he couldn't get in, Glam climbed up the walls, sat on the very top of the roof and rode the house. The zombie rocked the roof and shook the house, and roared and screamed, so no one could sleep inside.

Then, one night, Thorhall's new shepherd was late coming down from the hills, and he was killed by the angry zombie as the sun went down.

Word spread of this new haunting, this dangerous new zombie who was riding the roof of Thorhallsstead every night. No one would work for Thorhall now, so he considered taking his family away and abandoning the farm.

Then Grettir, a strong young man who wanted to be a famous young man, arrived at the farmhouse and asked if he could stay the night.

Thorhall shook his head. "We have a bit of a zombie problem at night."

"I know. I want to get rid of your zombie for you."

So Thorhall invited Grettir to stay the night. As the sun set, Grettir told the family to hide in the furthest corners of the house. Then he unbolted the front door and propped it open. He hid under a sheepskin, just inside the door, and waited.

Glam the zombie arrived outside. He climbed the house and rode on the roof, shaking the house so hard that dust fell from the ceiling and all the walls rattled.

Then the zombie slid down the roof and walked round the house, hitting the windows and groaning. Glam arrived at the open door. He stood for a moment, puzzled, his drooling mouth hanging open. Then he stepped inside.

Grettir leapt up from his hiding place, grabbed the zombie's cold clammy arms, and tried to fling him to the floor.

But Glam was strong with the power of death, and he fought back.

The two of them, the living and the dead, wrestled and fought in the farmhouse, tripping over rugs, rolling round the fire, knocking over barrels of beer and flour.

Glam tried to drag Grettir out of the house, but Grettir braced his feet on the stone doorstep and resisted with all his weight and strength. Suddenly Grettir lifted his feet, so that the zombie was pulling hard against nothing. The zombie lost his balance and fell outside into the moonlight.

Grettir landed hard on top of the zombie. Grettir used his weight and strength to pin the zombie to the ground, just long enough to draw his knife, then he sliced off the zombie's head.

Grettir laid the zombie's severed head beside the zombie's buttocks, to break the power of death. "Now you can rest," he said.

And Thorhall, stepping out of the farmhouse, added, "We can even make sure you're warm."

Then Grettir and Thorhall burnt Glam's motionless body to ashes.

Grettir left the farm the next morning with a new name, Grettir the Strong, and the beginning of his own saga.

Now that Thorhallsstead's most powerful ghost had been defeated, there were no more hauntings, so Thorhall could hire more farmworkers and start farming again. And the first thing he did was fix his roof.

# Hunting Magnus

from Magnus' Saga the Longer

There's a beautiful red cathedral in Kirkwall called St Magnus Cathedral, which was built almost 900 years ago to honour Orkney's first saint, St Magnus.

Magnus didn't always act like a saint. When he was young, he acted like most young Norse men, and went off 'viking'. He sailed round the British coast with the Norwegian king, raiding towns and villages, stealing and killing. The men of the north called this 'viking', so the people of these islands called them Vikings.

One evening, Magnus sat on the deck of the longship, looking over the water at the coast of Wales, and he said, "I have no quarrel with any man here. Why should I fight them?"

The other warriors on the ship laughed at him. But the king was angry with him. "You will fight because you are a Viking, and because I order you to fight."

As Magnus lay on deck under his blanket that night, he realised that if he stayed on the ship he would have to fight someone the next morning. He would have to fight the Welsh or he would have to fight the king.

So he slipped out from under his blanket, slipped over the side of the longship, and swam quietly away. As he reached the shore, he cut his ankle on a sharp rock and limped inland.

The next morning, the king yelled, "Where is Magnus? Let's make a man out of that boy. He will fight at my right hand today!"

But no one could find Magnus. He wasn't under his blanket, he wasn't anywhere on the ship. The king took his men ashore to hunt for Magnus, and they brought their dogs with them.

Magnus heard the warriors shouting and the dogs barking. He hadn't travelled far inland because he was limping, so he climbed up a tree to hide.

One of the dogs found a trail of blood and tracked Magnus to the tree.

Magnus looked down and the dog looked up. The dog opened its mouth to bark. Magnus snapped a branch from the tree and threw it.

But he didn't throw the stick *at* the dog, he threw it *for* the dog. The dog ran off through the woods, chasing the stick.

The dog ran to the king with the stick in its mouth, wagging its tail. The king said, "Stupid animal, it's not a game." He kicked the dog and walked off to search somewhere else.

So the King of Norway didn't find Magnus that morning. He soon gave up searching and sailed off to raid elsewhere.

Magnus made his long, slow, painful journey home to Orkney, where he became the islands' Earl, then the islands' saint.

And he never again fought a man he had no quarrel with.

# Odin's Riddles

from The Saga of King Heidrek the Wise

King Heidrek was so clever that he was called King Heidrek the Wise. One day he decreed that he would grant royal favour to any man who could ask him a riddle he couldn't answer.

Gestumblindi had been an opponent of Heidrek for a long time, even before Heidrek was crowned by the new bishop. Now that his old enemy was king, Gestumblindi was keen to be back in his favour. But Gestumblindi was useless at composing riddles.

So Gestumblindi made a sacrifice to Odin, the Father of the Old Gods, and asked for his help.

Odin came to Gestumblindi's door, and borrowed his hat, his cloak, his face and his voice. Then Odin travelled to the king's hall, announced himself as Gestumblindi, and said he would ask the king riddles to win his favour.

King Heidrek smiled. "Go on then, ask me a riddle."

Odin asked:

"Who sleeps lonely in the hearth pit?
*Born from stone and wood,*
*He has no parents to care for him,*
*He's bright and eager to leave,*
*But he'll live his life in the pit.*

Who is he?
Answer me this, O wise Heidrek."

Heidrek nodded. "That's a good riddle. You surprise me with your wit, Gestumblindi. But I have the answer. Fire lives in the hearth. He is made from flint and firewood, and I hope he will never get out! I doubt you have any riddles that can fool me."

So Odin asked:

"What is the creature,

Friend to us both at times,

That has a gory back,

And holds a man safe

In its hollow hand.

Answer me this, O wise Heidrek."

"It's a shield, covered in blood from the battle, but sheltering its holder," Heidrek said. "Don't you have any better riddles?"

So Odin asked:

"Women who sleep on a hard bed,

Who do not stir when the weather is still,

But who wake in the wind.

They put on their white hoods,

Then walk amongst the skerries.

Who are they?

Answer me this, O wise Heidrek."

Heidrek smiled. "A pretty picture, of the waves as women with white hoods blown by the wind. But not pretty enough to fool me."

So Odin asked:

> "Four are hanging,
>
> Four are walking,
>
> Two are pointing the way.
>
> And one, ever dirty, dangles behind.
>
> What is it?
>
> Answer me this, O wise Heidrek."

Heidrek laughed. "Not such a pretty picture, of a cow and her filthy tail! Don't take up my whole day with simple riddles."

So Odin asked:

> "What strange marvel
>
> Did I see outside your door?
>
> Eight feet, four eyes,
>
> And knees above its belly.
>
> Answer me this, O wise Heidrek."

Heidrek sighed. "It's a spider. And when great men sink to speaking of tiny spiders, they have spoken too long."

So Odin asked:

> "What has
>
> Six legs,
>
> Four eyes,
>
> Two heads,

And only one tail?

Answer me this, O wise Heidrek.”

“That’s a horse, with a rider. You’re beginning to bore me, Gestumblindi.”

“Then, wise king, what is this?

What has

Ten legs,

Three eyes,

Two heads,

And one tail?

Have you ever seen that?

Answer me this, O wise Heidrek.”

Heidrek frowned. “I have not seen that, because the answer is the false pagan god, one-eyed Odin, on his monstrous eight-legged horse Sleipnir. And he has left the world forever, pushed out by the truth of the new God. Your riddles are insultingly easy. You must challenge me with harder riddles, if you want to win this contest and win my favour back.”

“Then, Heidrek, answer me this, if you are truly wiser than any other king:

What did Odin whisper

In the ear of bright Baldur,

As the Lord of the Sun died

With his brother’s weapon in his heart?

Answer me that, O wise Heidrek.”

The king put his hand on the hilt of his sword. "I'm wise enough to know that no one has the answer to that question, except dead Baldur and fading Odin. And I'm wise enough to know who you really are, you old devil."

King Heidrek stood up and drew his sword. "You are no longer welcome here."

Odin turned into a hawk, and swooped around the hall.

The king threw his sword at the bird, and sliced off the end of the hawk's tail as it flew out of the hall.

So that is why hawks have a short straight-edged tail. That is why Gestumblindi never regained King Heidrek's favour. And that is why Odin and his family are not often seen in the northern lands these days.

# Where I Found These Stories:

There are many excellent translations of the sagas. I note the versions I used as my main sources below. Though the sagas were written down hundreds of years ago, many of them were based on stories which had been told out loud by storytellers for generations before that. The retellings I've collected in this book are the versions I tell out loud in schools, libraries and festivals. So these stories are not identical to the written sagas, they're my adaptations, changed to make sense in my voice and for young audiences. Several of these stories are expanded from small snippets which caught my eye in much longer sagas. And a few are shortened versions of sagas which contain slightly too much information about family trees!

## The Dragon's Hoard (set in Denmark)

This dragon story is from an utterly wonderful, extremely violent and rather nasty saga called the Volsung Saga, which contains lots of incredible stories, most of which I wouldn't tell to my own kids or even to my mum. But everyone likes a dragon story, especially one with a guest appearance by Loki. And Sigurd, who makes some very daft decisions later in his life, does come up with a good way to kill a dragon.

(Main source: *The Saga of the Volsungs*, translated by Jesse L Byock, Penguin Books, 1999)

## The Swan Warrior (set in Sweden)

There are lots of strong women in the Viking sagas, but most of them aren't very nice people. I like Kara's courage in using her magic to protect Helgi, and I also like that this story doesn't have a happy ending. Viking sagas don't often have fairy tale endings! Helgi and Kara's story is only a few lines in a saga about other characters, so I've expanded their tale to tell it to audiences.

(Main source: *The Saga of Hromund Gripsson*, translated by Ben Waggoner, in *Six Sagas of Adventure*, Troth Publications, 2014)

## The Berserker's Baby (set in Iceland)

Not all Viking warriors are nasty violent men. Some of them are also babysitters. This was one of the more unusual stories I found in the sagas. I changed it a little, letting Thorir talk to the sun god direct rather than getting someone else to do it for him, and also the original saga doesn't mention potty training!

(Main source: *The Saga of the People of Vatnsdal*, translated by Andrew Wawn, in *The Sagas of the Icelanders*, Penguin Classics, 2001)

## Tusker versus the Earl (set in Orkney and Scotland)

This was the first Viking saga story I ever told. I wanted to share it because I'm from Moray in the North East of Scotland, so when I tell the story of this attempted invasion of the mainland of Scotland, I tell it from the perspective of someone whose family and lands were attacked by the Vikings. I have no sympathy for that handsome Earl at all!

(Main source: *The Orkneyinga Saga*, translated by Hermann Palsson and Paul Edwards, Penguin Books, 1981)

## The Bear in Chains (set in Iceland, Greenland, Norway and Denmark)

This is probably the saga story I've changed the most. I just couldn't leave that poor bear stuck in a cage. The original tale of Audun is mostly concerned with how fortunate and rich Audun became, and doesn't even mention what happened to the bear after the king gave Audun all those gifts. So I decided to think about the story from the bear's point of view, and find a way to get the bear home that fitted the story.

(Main source: *The Tale of Audun from the West Fjords*, translated by Anthony Maxwell, in *The Sagas of the Icelanders*, Penguin Classics, 2001)

### The Raven Banner (set in Orkney, Scotland and Ireland)

This tale must have been told round firesides for years, because it appears in slightly different forms in a couple of different sagas. It's one of three stories in this collection about men called Sigurd: the Sigurd who killed the dragon, the handsome Earl Sigurd who duelled with Maelbrigte Tusker, and this Orkney Earl with the raven banner, who was actually named Sigurd the Stout. I haven't used the name Sigurd in all three stories, in case readers think they were all the same (very busy) man!

(Main source: *The Orkneyinga Saga*, translated by Hermann Palsson and Paul Edwards, Penguin Books, 1981; also *Njal's Saga*, translated by Carl F Bayerschmidt and Lee M Hollander, Wordsworth Editions, 1998).

### The Boy in the Bones (set in Denmark)

This is possibly my favourite saga story, and Bodvar is definitely my favourite Viking hero. I love his trick for making Hott look good and feel better about himself. Cate James and I had to invent the monster's shape, with the help of various schools in Fife and Edinburgh, because the saga doesn't give many details about what it looks like!

(Main source: *The Saga of King Hrolf Kraki*, translated by Jesse L Byock, Penguin Classics, 1998)

### Sailing to America (set in Iceland, Greenland, Norway and North America)

When I was a child and first heard that the Vikings had been to America before Columbus, I didn't believe it! It's now accepted as historical fact (you probably already knew) and the main source for information about the Vikings' voyages to North America are the Icelandic sagas. As my story is based on the sagas, it's focused on the Viking invaders. But I don't feel too sorry for Thorvald. Remember what they did to the men hiding under the boats…

(Main source: *The Greenlanders' Saga*, in *The Vinland Sagas*, translated by Magnus Magnusson and Hermann Palsson, Penguin Books, 1965)

### Zombie on the Roof (set in Iceland)

I'm often asked by readers at author events if I'll ever write a book about zombies, and I've always said, 'No, probably not,' to their great disappointment. So I'm delighted to have the chance to put a zombie in a book. Vikings may not have called their ghosts zombies, but Glam was definitely one of the living, walking dead. And I love that the way to defeat him was to place his severed head beside his buttocks. This story is great fun to tell (but not to very young children…)

(Main source: *Grettir's Saga*, translated by Jesse Byock, Oxford University Press, 2009)

### Hunting Magnus (set in Orkney and Wales)

Like many of the characters in these sagas, Magnus was a real person who can also be found in history books. I'm not sure how historically true this story is, but he definitely wasn't your typical young Viking warrior. The idea of throwing the stick to distract the dog wasn't his idea though. That came from one of my daughters when I was telling her this story. Like many sagas, this story has lots of people with the same name – the king that Magnus of Orkney wouldn't fight for was called Magnus Barelegs!

(Main source: *Magnus' Saga the Longer*, in *Icelandic Sagas*, Vol 3, translated by George W Dasent, Eyre and Spottiswoode, 1894)

### Odin's Riddles (set in Sweden)

I love this story for its riddles, though I did simplify and reword most of them. Did you get the answers before King Heidrek? There are dozens more riddles in the original saga, some of which are impossible to answer unless you're a Viking. If you tell this story to anyone else, perhaps you could make up your own riddles…

(Main source: *The Saga of King Heidrek the Wise*, translated by Christopher Tolkien, Harper Collins, 2010)

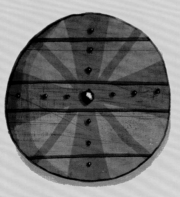